Snake Bit

Snake Bit

Snake Bit

Copyright © 2023 by Kelly M. Goodrich

For further information on mail-order sales, wholesale or retail discounts, and distribution please contact the publisher.

K. M. Goodrich
KGMarkets@gmail.com
www.KMGRealtor.com

First Edition October 2023

ISBN

Printed in the U.S.A.

Snake Bit

This story is dedicated to Laurie, my best wife and our friends that rode the trails with us, these rides and these friends inspired the Hutch stories.

"All you all" know who you are!

Thanks for all of the great times on the trail and around the fire.

Kelly M. Goodrich.

Snake Bit
Contents

Snake Bit

Snake Bit

Introduction

The Hutch stories are based in the mid-1890's in Territorial Arizona on the fictitious Dove Valley Ranch. The Dove Valley Ranch lies South of the very small town of Cave Creek with its northwest corner about two miles south at Cave Creek Road and runs east to the Verde River and south to modern day Deer Valley Road with the western boundary following Cave Creek Road.

Cave Creek started out as a cavalry remount station in 1870's called Cave Creek Station. Miners came into the area in the mid 1870's when gold was discovered around Black Mountain. Cave Creek Road was established as a wagon trail to connect Cave

Snake Bit

Creek to Phoenix. Cattle ranchers settled in the area around Cave Creek in the 1880's. The map of Arizona for 1887 shows Cave Creek Station and the Arizona map for 1895 shows Cave Creek with the Station dropped.

Most small towns were settled because there was a dependable source of water, Cave Creek is no different. The cavalry needed water for their horses, that source of water was the Cave Creek stream. Cave Creek stream is fed water from the rain runoff from Black mountains. The runoff also charges local springs that provide a source of water throughout the year.

Cave Creek was very much a Miner/Cowtown during the mid-1890s. Cave Creek experienced all of the problems that many small western towns like Cave Creek went through at the time including; saloons, gambling and prostitution.

By 1895 the Railroad connected Phoenix to the Atlantic and Pacific Railroad at Ashfork in northern Arizona by way of Prescott and southwest to Wickenburg. Phoenix was also connected to the Southern Pacific Railroad in southern Arizona with a spur from Maricopa, allowing Phoenix to grow and prosper while Cave Creek remained a small town just trying to survive.

This story weaves a tale through one of the productive prospecting areas of Arizona. The

Snake Bit

Phoenix Mining Company first opened the Phoenix Mine, and later opened the nearby Maricopa Mine. See the exhibit below, it is a copy of the original filing for the Maricopa Mine. Greed has a way of taking over people and gold fever has been known to be deadly. Gold fever was so deadly in Arizona that after the Indian wars had been settled the Army was reassigned to protect prospectors and mining operations.

When there is a successful Gold Mine Claim they are usually found in the hills and mountains. Water was required for any successful mining operation. As the water was used at the mines it flowed into washes, creeks and streams. Placer Miners would file claims downstream from mines, using pans to separate gold from mud. Gold was also rinsed downstream by the rain from the tailings or materials that the miners removed from the mine and set aside. Mine owners often considered the gold that rinsed downstream to be theirs. These Mine owners would do their best to chase off the Placer Miners. Greed flourished where the law had limited reach and resources. This is often where the best stories begin.

Hutch and his friends have the opportunity to find adventure and trouble around every bend. My only hope is that you enjoy reading about Hutch and

Snake Bit

his friends as much as I have enjoyed writing about Hutch's adventures.

The Hutch stories are fiction, all of the characters are a figment of my imagination.

Kelly M. Goodrich.

Snake Bit

This is a copy of a Mining Claim filed in 1885 in the Cave Creek Mining District.

LOT NO. 37 A & B

SURVEY NO. 752 & 753

Field Notes

of the survey of the

Maricopa Mining Claim

and Phoenix Millsite

Situate in _Cave Creek_ Mining District

County of _Maricopa_ and in Sec _____, Tp _____ 1 N

Range _____ 4 E, of the Gila and Salt River Meridian.

ARIZONA.

Claimed by _Phoenix Mining Company_

Survey executed by _Herbert R Patrick_ D. S.

Under instructions dated _June 1st_ 1885

Survey commenced _December 15th_ 1885

Survey completed _" 17th_ 1885

11

Snake Bit

Now in Hutch's own words.

One

"Thanks" Josh Harmen said to Assayer as he put his new found cash in his pocket and stepped out of the Assayer's office and onto the boardwalk. Josh Harmen had just cashed in his gold pannings after about 5 weeks of hard work. Josh was tired and dirty, he needed a bath and a shave before he went to see his family at the Diner and Bakery. As Josh stepped off of the boardwalk a Stranger in town, stepped from the side of the building that housed the

Snake Bit

Assayer's office, the stranger was tall and slender, dark haired from what you could see under his hat, two days worth of dark stubble on his face. He had a wicked interest in the miner. He followed the miner from a distance, he took notice as the miner crossed the street and stepped into the Barber Shop. The Stranger went into the saloon attached to the hotel across the street from the Barber Shop. He got a bottle from the Bartender and took a seat by the window to keep an eye on the Barber Shop. The miner came out of the Barber Shop clean with a fresh shave and haircut. He continued on the boardwalk to his right, one door down, and went into the Harmen Diner and Bakery. The Stranger watched the miner as he stepped into the Diner and waited for him to come out. Josh greeted his wife Maria and daughter Sara as he stepped into the Diner. His wife and daughter came for a hug. Josh asked "where are the boys?"

"They are out hunting. How did the panning go?"

Josh reached into his pocket and pulled out a wad of cash, handed it to her and said "okay".

Maria took the cash and said "this will hold us over for awhile". Then Maria asked, "how long are you staying?"

Josh replied "I gotta get back tomorrow, the gold won't wait".

Snake Bit

Maria whispered with a smile "I see you got a bath, I will do all I can to make you comfortable tonight".

Maria made him a filling meal of fresh bolillos, beans and a steak. After Josh finished his meal he pushed back from the table and asked his wife for a pencil and paper. Josh made a list of the supplies he would need for the next two weeks. When Josh was done with the list, he handed it to his daughter Sara and asked her to take it next door to the Hutchinson General Store. Please tell Cherish that I will pick up the order in the morning. Maria handed Sara enough money to cover the order.

Maria told Sara to get something for herself. Times had been tough for the Harmon's, running a Diner and Bakery in a small town was not very profitable.   Recently, the Phoenix Mine shut down, but the Maricopa mine hit a large vein of gold. Men that lost jobs at the Phoenix filed Placer claims on any stream, creek or wash with running water. Josh followed suit, it was just the boost that the family needed.

The Stranger watching from across the street, saw a beautiful young girl come from the Diner and headed next door to the Hutchinson General Store. The Stranger waited all day and the miner had not come out. Shortly after the girl returned the lantern in the front of the Diner and Bakery went out, the miner was in for the night.

The Stranger gave up his perch near the window of the saloon after the lights had gone out across the street. He stepped into the hotel, he asked for a room on the North side so he could keep watch. He went into the small hotel dining room and got dinner. After dinner, he went to his room. He moved the chair over to the window and took up watch and promptly fell asleep.

The next morning, the sun came through the Stranger's window and warmed the room. He stretched and decided the chair had not been the best place to sleep. He was surprised when he looked out and noticed the young girl from the Diner and Bakery as she tied a horse to the rail in front of the Diner and disappeared inside. Shortly after, the miner stepped out and made his way to the General Store. The miner reappeared with some packages that he put into his saddle bags. The miner mounted his horse and headed out of town.

The Stranger started getting ready for the day, he didn't need to rush, he knew where the miner was headed. After washing his face the Stranger went downstairs for breakfast in the Hotel dining room. Coffee, eggs, bacon, beans and a fresh roll probably from the Bakery across the street. With the last sip of coffee gone he headed to the Livery Stable to get his horse.

The Stranger headed west out of town on the Cave Creek Road until he reached a fork. He followed the west fork to take him to Cave Creek, the south fork turned toward Phoenix. When he reached Cave Creek he followed the creek north along its southern banks until he was about a quarter of a mile from the miners claim. In the Springtime, Cave Creek ran heavy with water from the snow melt and rain. In the slow summer it would slow to a babbling creek. The banks of Cave Creek were green with grasses, palo verde trees and creosote bushes offering the Stranger good cover and a quiet approach. The Stranger dismounted and tied his horse to a palo verde tree. He knew his horse could pull away if it had a mind to, but his horse was well trained and would stay put. On foot he followed the creek the rest of the way. When he came upon the miner, the miner was in the creek panning. The Stranger drew his gun.

The miner caught some movement out of his left eye and quickly drew his gun, but the Stranger was quicker. The miner shot, fell into the creek bleeding out. The Stranger didn't want others downstream to see the blood in the creek so the Stranger dragged the miner out of the creek. The Stranger searched the miners pockets and saddle bags for money and

Snake Bit

the claim. The miner didn't have any money but he found the claim. The Stranger didn't really care about the money, his boss just wanted the claim and the miner out of the way. Any money he took off the miner was his to keep.

Snake Bit

Two

"Turn that calf loose" Bill Roberts called out "that's enough for today." Dusk was settling in on the ranch. With one more pen of calves to be branded, they can wait till tomorrow.

"Hutch this branding chute you built is working pretty good, we are about a week ahead of schedule" Bill added. "You got any plans after the branding is done?" Bill asked?

"Dan won a gold claim on Cave Creek in a poker game in Wickenburg. I thought I would check in on him, see if he needs a hand" I replied.

"Dan, you mean Dan Kanten?" Bill asked?

"One in the same" I shot back.

Snake Bit

Bill replied "Nice enough guy but he seems to find his share of trouble. A gold claim ya say, I am surprised. The Dan Kanten I know would work his ass off to get out of work more than any man I know; I can't see him working a gold claim."

"I know, I am surprised too, but he's a good hand, so he must have done some work in the past."

"Where is this claim?

"It is on the Cave Creek, about 2 miles upstream from town. He pointed it out to me when we came back after turning in Rafe Baxter's body for the reward."

"You be careful up there, I heard there have been some problems in that area" Bill added.

"I hadn't heard that, I'll be careful".

Bill added "Tomorrow the branding will be done, Captain Brown ordered twenty head of cattle and 6 horses to be delivered to Fort Whipple near Prescott in about four weeks. If you are back in time?"

"I sure don't intend to take up prospecting, I'll be back".

"We are a bit short handed if Dan is done playing with his gold claim by then, we could use him on the drive."

"You and I both know that prospecting doesn't suit him, I will check with him,".

Snake Bit

"Andrea is coming home tomorrow, so after the branding is done we're going to roast a pig and have a party to celebrate her graduation. Would you pick out one of the weaned pigs from the pen and get it ready" Bill asked?

Andrea, Bill and Leanne's only daughter, had been attending Arizona Normal School, a Teachers college in Tempe Arizona.

"Yes sir, anything else?"

"Before we start branding tomorrow morning, get that pig cooking in the pit, Winnie will take care of everything else. I will send Tim over to help you with the pig" Bill added.

"We'll get it done" I shot back.

I returned to my cabin to get my gun, by the time I got to the pigpen, Tim was already there. Tim was the only person I knew that seemed to like killing. When we were younger we would go hunting, Tim would lose track of what we were hunting and just start shooting at anything that moved. When my family first came to the Arizona territory hunting was a necessity, if I didn't make a kill we wouldn't have meat for the table. I thanked God and said a prayer of thanks every time I made a kill. The thought of any animal suffering at my hand really hurts me. Tim on the other hand seemed to take pleasure in the kill, more than once I caught him just standing over a dove he'd shot watching as it flopped around on the ground. I'd move in and grab the bird and immediately take its head off to stop the suffering. Tim thought I was a killer like him, he called me "Cold" short for Cold Blooded, but I can't bare to watch an animal suffer. When I killed Rafe Baxter it was him or me, no time to think about it. When you kill a man he is gone, you are left to deal with your actions, just because it was justified doesn't mean it won't bother you. I think Tim was missing something inside, I think that's why he is always getting in trouble. Anyway, I can tell Tim wants to take the shot to put the pig down, I'll let them, I'll be ready with my knife just in case the kill shot wasn't clean.

We picked out a nice healthy pig, big enough to feed twenty to thirty people. I sorted him out and pushed him into a smaller pen. Tim lined up the shot and squeezed the trigger, the pig dropped right there. I moved in and cut its throat so it would bleed out quickly. We hung and gutted the pig then we prepared it for the spit and let it rest overnight.

Three

I was up at dawn, the eastern sun pierced through the clouds over Four Peaks, the light of the sun cast an orange and red hue, it was my favorite time on Dove Valley Ranch. The quiet was calming and peaceful, there was a chill in the morning air, I used this time to plan my day. I washed my face and dressed quickly. and headed for the cooking pit. I started a fire in the pit to get a nice bed of coals, then I headed to the bunkhouse, Winnie had coffee and breakfast ready. The coffee was hot and strong, if I wasn't awake before, I was wide awake after a cup of Winnie's coffee. Bacon, I helped cure, scrambled eggs, refried beans and tortillas, all my favorites filled out the morning plate.

After breakfast, I went to check on the coals, they were looking good so I spread them out and added more wood. Tim made his way down to the fire pit together we got the pig secured on the spit, then we moved it over the fire. Ricardo Roberts, we call him Ric, Tim's younger half brother came down to keep an eye on the pig and turn it regularly so it wouldn't burn. Tim and I went to the branding pen. We had one more pen of calves to brand, then I would be off for a few days. The coals from yesterday's branding still had a glow, I added some more wood on the coals and worked the bellows. The coals were bright red, and in no time at all we were ready to start. I put the branding iron on the coals and Tim pushed the first calf into the shoot. Head after head we pushed the calves into the chute. Wide leather straps pulled them snug against one side of the chute so they wouldn't struggle as we applied the brand. We released the straps and opened the chute gate and Buster would nip at their heels and out they'd run. Buster was one dog that knew his job, he seemed to love working cattle. The branding chute was my winter project, I worked on it between hunting trips and ranch work. I got the idea for the chute the previous spring, when it was clear that the ranch hands couldn't handle a rope

Snake Bit

worth a damned, there had to be an easier way. We used pinch pens to doctor injured animals in the past. The pinch pen just used an extra panel to trap an animal against the side of a stall. My branding chute was just a stall with wide leather straps to bind the animal to one side of the stall. The last pen of calves went quickly and so did the morning.

Bill Roberts made it a practice to round up his herd and drive them back to the large holding pens around the ranch headquarters for branding. Bill would take a head count and determine what he could sell off and what he needed to keep to insure the health of the herd. The first year calves were branded and turned out for the summer. Bull calves would be castrated if they didn't figure into the breeding plans. By the time the steers were two years old they were ready to go to market. Some of the steers would be sold locally, some would be sold to the Army Posts and the rest would be driven to the stockyards in Phoenix. The cattle that went to the stockyards were often sold wholesale and put on the train to be sent to Chicago or St. Louis for processing and distribution. Anyway, the branding chute worked well and this year the branding was done a week ahead of schedule.

Dove Valley Ranch sits near the banks of the Verde River North and West of Fort McDowell and runs to Cave Creek Trail on the West; the Northwest

Snake Bit

corner is at Cave Creek Trail about 2 miles south of Cave Creek. The South border of the Roberts Ranch is somewhere around Deer Valley about 15 miles north of Phoenix city limits.   The ranch was not completely fenced so the boundaries didn't really matter, the cattle were branded and they would roam wherever they could find grass and water. In early Spring the ranch hands would ride out in different directions to push the cattle back onto the ranch and into ranch holding pens for branding.   Sure, Bill would lose a few head of cattle every year to mountain lions, Indians and rustlers. Bill didn't mind losing the occasional steer to the Indians or mountain lions, they would only take what they needed.   The rustlers on the other hand needed to be driven to ground and run off.

Bill Roberts moved his family here from New Mexico.   Bill fled New Mexico during the Lincoln County Wars where he worked for Legendary Cattleman John Chisum. The ranch started out as a one room shack, today the ranch house is a single story home with four bedrooms, an office, a large sitting room and dining room. In the Southwest corner of the home, the kitchen and a bedroom made into an office were all that is left of the original adobe shack.   The whole house is wrapped with a porch. The wrap around porch had doors from each bedroom that allowed the family to move outside on

Snake Bit

hot summer nights.   At times you could see Bill Roberts sitting on the porch in his big rocking chair watching the workings of the ranch.

The bunkhouse for the hands was built around 1890, it could sleep up to ten hands when needed. The kitchen is separate from the bunkhouse and it has separate quarters for the ranch cook, Winnie and her husband Rice live there when he is not in jail. The hands would eat outside when weather permitted otherwise they would eat in the bunkhouse. The bunkhouse grew in proportion along with the ranch. Several pens were located south of the bunkhouse where the hands kept their horses including their strings.   Each hand had to work a string of horses after the rest of the ranch work was done.   Bill would pay them a bonus when their horses were sold if they had a good handle. There is a large barn with several stalls, it sits to the west of the bunkhouse for broodmares and Bill's favorite horses.   Just north of the barn separated by the trail leading off the ranch to Cave Creek Trail there are three large corrals where the cows and calves are brought for branding. We also use the corrals to separate the cattle going to market. Immediately north of the large corral there were several smaller pens used as branding pens. The large corrals are also used to work the colts, the corral could be seen from the porch at the big house where Bill could watch the hands work the colts. If Bill caught one of the hands mistreating the colts he would be run off immediately.

My cabin and Queenie's stall are situated on a mostly flat area about three hundred feet east of the bunkhouse and south of Ranch house.

Throughout the day, I would take short breaks to check on Ric as he tended the pig as it cooked over the fire pit. He was doing a good job keeping the coals stoked but making sure the flames didn't burn the pig.

Ric is Bill's youngest son, his mother Marianna died giving birth to him. In the early years life on Dove Valley Ranch was hard and Bill's wife Leanne had a difficult time, she chose to return to her family in New Mexico. With Leanne gone Marianna took over the household duties. Bill didn't know if Leanne would ever return. Bill was lonely, he and Marianna grew close and one not so lonely night Ricardo was conceived. Marianna had a very difficult time and passed away after giving birth to Ric. After Marianna had passed, Leanne returned to Dove Valley Ranch and took up her duties beside Bill and raised Ric as her own child.

Ric and Tim were as different as night and day. Tim had to be told to do something while Ric would jump in and try to help out without being asked. Ric was smart and quick to learn while Tim was slow and

Snake Bit

lazy.   Tim acted as though the Ranch was his birthright while Ric wanted to learn everything he could about ranching.

As we wrapped up the branding I noticed a one horse buggy pull onto the ranch and head to the ranch house, Andrea was home from school. The prodigal daughter returns for a grand celebration.

Four

Andrea was not what you would call beautiful but she was an attractive girl with long fine hair the color of oat hay a little darker than the mane of a palomino. Where the classic beauties left off she filled in nicely, she was built a little closer to the ground maybe topping out at 5 feet. Her blue eyes were filled with light, and her smile would brighten any room. When she left for school she was a skinny little girl, but from a distance I could see she filled out her clothing with plenty of curves. She didn't have a long slender neck or a long mid waist, she had a fine figure fit for any endeavor. She was a fireball full of energy and mischief. Andrea often followed me around the ranch, I kinda liked it but never let her know, in fact I would shue her away often. Bill always made me feel like I was a part of the family and I wouldn't feel right to think of her as anything more than a sister, so I made a point of keeping her at arm's length.

Bill made a practice of throwing a spring feast at Easter, and Andrea's Graduation made it more special. The pig was almost cooked, it was time to help Ric get it off of the fire. Some of the town folk were arriving, friends of the Roberts family, including my mother Cherish, my sister Kate and brother Ed. My older brother Frank Jr. must be watching the store. The ranch hands were setting up tables in the yard in front of the ranch house, then came the red and white checkered tablecloths, then the silverware and fresh cut flowers including desert star and desert sunflower at the table centers. There was a three piece band setting up on the front porch. The stage was set for a big celebration, this was going to be a spring feast to remember. This would be a grand affair, I think I will let this party pass without me.

I helped Winnie and the ranch hands bring dinner to the tables. The tables were set and I turned to leave Winnie grabbed my butt, I whipped around and asked "where's Rice tonight?"

Winnie replied "he is in jail, why don't you come by later."

"Yea, that's not going to happen. What did Rice do now?"

Snake Bit

"He got into a fight, somebody had to go to the doctor, but it wasn't Rice," Winnie commented, almost proud of the fact that her husband didn't kill someone.

"Yea, it seems like it's always someone else that gets hurt. I am sure one of the ranch hands will help you out tonight. I am heading out in the morning so I am turning in early".

"Well they ain't you, but I guess one of them will do." Winnie went on to ask "Are you heading through town?"

"Yup, I'll be stopping at the general store for some supplies" I answered.

"Would you stop by the Marshal's office and give something to Rice for me?" Winnie asked.

"Yea, I'll stop by, I gotta talk to Jake anyway. I will come by in the morning for some breakfast before I head out, you can give it to me then."

Winnie was a homely woman with heavy breasts that hung low, her hair was seldom combed. To look at her, she had no features that gave evidence of national origin, but with a name like Wilma her family likely came from Germanic Europe. As unattractive as she was, she could not be satisfied by her husband Rice. Rice was the ranch foreman for a time, but he hurt a couple of the hands and Bill demoted him. Rice is a deadly man with a jealous streak. I have heard many stories about the razor

31

Snake Bit

that Rice wheeled and that blade came out most often when he found Winnie with another man. When new hands were hired, Bill let them know that it was best to stay away from Winnie, they took one look at her and thought to themselves no problem. But, Winnie has a way of getting the boys to come around, she keeps after them with a flash of her breasts or a lewd comment and in a weak moment they'd give in. If they were lucky Rice wouldn't find out, but most can't wait to tell their story in the bunk house and it always seems to find its way back to Rice and another ranch hand would disappear. Rice didn't blame Wilmal, she had needs, they were trespassing. I don't know why Bill hasn't chased Rice off, I think Winnie has some dirt on Bill or maybe he was just a loyal friend.

I grabbed some dinner with the other ranch hands at the bunkhouse, then headed for my cabin. I packed my saddle bags with ammo and clean change of clothes and other essentials. I cleaned and loaded my rifle and checked my sidearm and I was ready for bed. I stoked the fire in my little stove and undressed for bed. After a long day of branding and party preparations I was worn out. As soon as I hit the bed I was gone.

What seemed like a couple hours passed and I was comfortably sleeping when I woke to a knock on the cabin door, Buster growled.

Snake Bit

"Yea, who's there?" I asked.

"It's Andrea, let me in before someone sees me out here."

I pulled my pants on and slipped on a shirt, too groggy to button up.

"What are you doing here Andrea?".

"I didn't see you at the spring feast."

"I wasn't invited," I replied.

"Since when do you need an invitation, you're part of the family?"

"I had a long day and I am heading out in the morning and I thought I would turn in early."

"I visited with your ma, she is so sweet. she seemed to think you were having trouble with your brothers."

"Yea, I had words with Frank over some short trading he did with a poor farming family, but that's another story" I replied.

"I've graduated and I am moving into town to teach at the Indian School. I will be living in the teacher's dorms at the school. You know you learn a lot at college, girls talk, we share our experiences."

"Andrea, what are you doing here?".

Subtly, Andrea slipped her warm hands inside of my shirt and around my waist and said "I had a crush on you for as long as I can remember, I came to see you."

Snake Bit

I could feel her warm hand on my back, still half asleep, I was caught by surprise as Andrea moved in to kiss me. I thought of Andrea as a kid sister, slowing my response, but I did my best to catch up. She pressed her curves against my body and before I knew it my shirt was on the floor and we were wrapped in a heated embrace. Andrea's hands were moving quickly and I responded in kind as we explored each other's body. She was once an awkward kid, she has turned into a mountain lion that would not be turned away. Thoughts of her father and what he would say moved in and out of my head but she would not be denied. I tried to push her away, but not too hard, as she returned for more. I was lost the second her warm hand made its way into my jeans. I could not take her clothes off fast enough, my hands found her firm warm breasts. Andrea slid my pants to the floor and pushed me towards the bed. We were naked. As I sat down on the bed, she leaned into me and I laid back on the bed. I slowed to take a breath and enjoy the moment, that didn't last long, the cat was on the move as she trapped me beneath her. We moved in rhythm, our bodies were working together towards one end. I felt her moisture, but I could tell that I wasn't inside her and as I tried to move in that direction she moved away saying "settle down cowboy." I laid back and let her run the show. The intimate contact that she allowed did not diminish my pleasure, she made sure of that. She moved against me slowly at first, then suddenly she began to move faster. I could not keep up, quicker and quicker. Then a soft slow moan came from Andrea and I lost it. Andrea was satisfied and she made sure I was too. She laid down on my chest for a few minutes to catch her breath. She got out of bed and went to the table where I had a washbowl with fresh water and towels set up for the morning. Fire from the stove lit her silhouette, her hips and firm breasts were well proportioned, her curves were breathtaking. She washed herself as I watched, she teased with every move. Then, in the moment, she turns and steps into her dress, pulling it up from the floor, playing the bashful girl. She pulled herself together quickly. Then she came to me where I lay on the bed watching her. She kissed me on the forehead, she moved to the door and slipped into the dark of night. I could not help but feel I had just been dismissed by the new teacher, well I think she taught me something new. On further thought it became clear to me this incident was very well rehearsed.

Andrea came at me like a train and while I enjoyed every second of it, I didn't feel like I had a choice. Most men would have taken full advantage of the situation without regard for her or her family.

Snake Bit

I am sure happy to be getting off the ranch first thing in the morning. I don't want to face her father and I hope he doesn't get wind of this. I can't stop the feeling that it was a betrayal of Bill's trust.

If asked, I could honestly say if she came into my cabin a virgin she was still a virgin when she left. I tossed and turned trying to wash my mind of the evening. Sleep didn't come easily that night, and when it did, it only came because I was dead tired.

Five

I woke at dawn as light filled the cabin. I moved quickly to pull myself together. I washed myself and threw on my clothes. I threw the door open, grabbed my saddle, saddle bags and tossed it over the hitching rail outside the door. I pulled Queenie from her pen, tied her to the rail with a feed bag so she could get to her fill of grain. I started to brush out her coat and mane as quickly as possible. Queenie got squirrely and tried to move away, she could tell something was bothering me. I stopped and took a deep breath. Queenie settled down and I continued patiently. Queenie was a good horse, she could do it all she was great on cattle and the trail.

Snake Bit

Bill Roberts gave me Queenie when she was a young filly. None of the ranch hands thought much of her, now they would trade anything to have her. I talked to her while I brushed, she seemed to like that. I got the saddle on her, snugged up the latigo, tied my bedroll and saddlebags and put my rifle in the scabbard. I took one more look in the cabin to make sure I didn't forget anything. Satisfied, I secured the cabin and walked Queenie to the bunkhouse for coffee and breakfast. I tied the feedbag with grain to Queenie's bridle so she could finish her breakfast. I went in for coffee, breakfast, fresh biscuits and bacon. Winnie put together a pack for my saddle bags, biscuits and jerky for the trail. She also handed me a package for Rice. I ate breakfast quickly and ran out forgetting the pack Winnie made for me. I wanted to get the hell off the ranch as soon as possible. Winnie ran out with the pack, wearing only her thin linen nightgown, with the sun behind her I saw more than I ever wanted to see. I thought to myself "now I got that stuck in my head". I took one more pull on the latigo and stepped into the saddle.

I rode out of the northwest gate onto Cave Creek road, Buster was close behind. Hell, I almost forgot about him. I took a biscuit and some bacon from my bag and offered it to him. I felt like a snake

Snake Bit

slithering off the ranch with the guilt of taking pleasure from Bill Roberts' only daughter. Bill took me in when I was having trouble with my family, he gave me a chance at life. I had always done my best to return his trust, but this time I crossed a line. I didn't think Andrea would say anything to her Father but I knew I had violated a code, it wasn't written, but it was something that I tried to live by. I need this trip to put some time and space between me and the ranch.

After Buster finished his breakfast he ran up in front. Queenie and I are in step but not moving as fast as Buster. Buster disappears up the road, after a minute or two I hear him barking. I squeezed my heels into Queenie's side and clicked my tongue to get her into stride. We catch up to Buster to find him barking at a rattlesnake sunning on the trail. It was still mid spring and mornings are still a bit nippy, so it is a surprise to see a snake out. Buster doesn't like snakes and he made sure I knew it was there. I could shoot it or just move off the trail past him. That morning I felt akin to the snake, so I moved past him like a good neighbor. It only served to remind me that last night I was the snake and my cabin was a snake pit. I called Buster off the rattler and we continued on down the road. Buster is a heck of a cattle dog, just ask him and he'll jump in and help with the stock. Since I got Buster from Leslie Graham he hasn't left my side. Buster's mother was an Australian Cattle Dog named Sheila. Buster's father was a lone coyote who was running across Leslie's ranch, he stopped just long enough to breed Sheila. Leslie raised the dogs for hunting and to work stock. Nobody in Payson would take a chance on a half breed coyote, Leslie couldn't put him down so he offered Buster to me. My trips off the ranch are made better by Buster and Queenie as my companions.

We were covering ground quickly that morning. Queenie had a gate between a walk and a trot and that pace allowed us to cover a lot of territory. Queenie was part Mustang and part Morgan, we wondered where the gate came from. We surmised over hours of discussion that the Mustangs must have been closely related to the gaited horses brought from Spain by Cortez.

Cave Creek Road began to curve to the east as the small town of Cave Creek came into view. On the north side of Cave Creek Road I could see my family's store, the Hutchinson General Store then the Harmen Diner and Bakery followed by the Barber Shop. Now all of main street Cave Creek came into view continuing on the north side of town he could see the Marshal's Office and the Livery Stable. The

Snake Bit

Marshal's office and Livery Stable had been built and abandoned by the Army, it served as a remount and watering station, its service is done. On the south side of the road sat the largest building in town, the Hotel, Saloon and a small dining room welcoming visitors from everywhere. Next a side street heading south into the small neighborhood of Cave Creek where most of the citizens of Cave Creek resided. Situated directly across Cave Creek Road from the Marshal's Office was the Bank and attached to the eastern wall of the bank was the Assayer's Office and Post Office. The post office sign was a new addition.

Six

It's too early to go to the family store, I guess I'll stop at the Hotel for some coffee. I tied Queenie to the rail in front of the hotel, Buster settled in near Queenie's front feet. I made my way to the hotel dining room. Marshal Jake Compton was sitting by the window eating breakfast and watching the street like a good Marshal should. I grabbed a cup of coffee from the buffet and moved to Jake's table. "Mind if I sit down" I asked?

Jake must have been deep in thought, he looked up at me with surprise "Hutch, please join me" he replied while kicking the chair out.

Snake Bit

I noticed that he was stewing on something so I asked "something bothering you?"

"This town is going to wear me out, we got rid of Baxter, the next thing you know somebody is killing off prospectors".

I was surprised, Bill warned me but he didn't have or provide me with any details. My first thought was Dan, I wondered if he was mixed up in the trouble in the mining district. Jake hadn't heard anything about Dan being in harm's way. What Jake did tell me was that one prospector disappeared and Josh Harman was found dead at this claim. A third prospector was found dead just off of the trail on the way back to his claim. The Phoenix Mining Company shut down operations last fall and the miners scattered. Some of the miners filed Placer Claims including Josh, others left for the next big gold find. The Placer Claims were located on the creeks downstream from the bigger mines. The rains would wash the tailings from the old mines downstream and some of the Gold went with it.

After my second cup of coffee, it was clear that Jake didn't know a whole lot more. Jake was a good man but he didn't seem to have a clue where to look or what to look for in this case, even if he did, he was undermanned, he didn't have a budget for deputies. From time to time he would deputize me, but I never got paid for it.

Snake Bit

"Jake, I got a care package for Rice from Winnie" I offered as I reached into my pocket.

"What is it, Hutch?"

"Not sure she asked me to give it to him, it ain't big enough to be a gun or a knife, I thought better of giving it to him, I figured I better give it to you."

Jake took the package "probably bail, that man gets into trouble every time he brings that razor out Hutch. One of these days he'll kill someone and I'll have to deal with it." Jake didn't know but the stories that follow Rice have him killing a couple of men with that razor.

"I know Jake, be careful."

I had an idea! My next stop would be the Assayer's Office before I headed out of town. Town was beginning to wake up so I took a short walk down the street.

I Thought it was early, but Herb Patrick was already at his desk at the Assayer's and Post Office. The Assayer's Office was not large, no place for visitors to sit, as you stepped into the office you were met with a short wall about four feet high and bars from the top of the wall to the ceiling. The bars had a slot that allowed items to be passed under the bars. On the counter there was a scale, behind the bars sat Herb's desk and behind that there was a

Snake Bit

large floor safe and a filing cabinet to the left of the safe. Further to the left was a new set of small mail slots. The territory was setting up the Assayer's office to double as the Post Office.

Herb looked up from his desk and asked "Hutch, how are you doing? Do you have some gold to sell?"

"No, but I do got some questions," I replied.

"What can I help you with?"

"Looks like the Assayer's office is turning into a post office?" The United States Postal Service has been making an effort to set up Post Offices across the Arizona territory, Cave Creek is the latest.

"The Assay business is slowing down, I think I can handle both, trying to keep busy." "The town folk decided I would be a good Postmaster, I hope I can live up to their expectations."

"Jake told me, one of the prospectors that were murdered was Josh Harman, what can you tell me about his claim" I asked"

"Josh had a placer claim on Cave Creek about 2 miles upstream from the town. He filed the claim about eight weeks ago and a few days ago he came in with a little over nine ounces of gold. Most of it flakes and dust but there were a couple of nice nuggets too. He was really happy, he left here with a pocket full of cash and coins".

Snake Bit

"Anybody come in asking about his claim" I pushed?

"No, but there was another miner that went missing, Joseph O'Malley brought in just over 5 ounces of gold then he never returned to his claim. About two weeks later a man came in with a O'Malley's claim and a bill of sale for the claim and I never heard another word from O'Malley" Herb answered. I had to transfer the claim because O'malley's signature was an X.

"What name did the new owner of the O'Malley claim give you?".

"Blake Haggard, never heard the name before" Herb replied.

"Where was O'Malley's claim?"

"You know these placer claims aren't very big, maybe 20 yards wide along the creek and 20 yards deep away from the creek." He paused for a second to recall "O'Malley's claim was Two claims up the creek from the Harman claim." "I got a claim map if you want to take a look."

"Yae, I'll take a look at it. What about the other prospector that was killed, what can you tell me about him?" I questioned.

"Jorge Shultz had a claim, I hadn't noticed it before, but you can see on the map, Shultz's claim was between the Harman claim and the O'Malley claim. I saw Shutz in town a couple weeks ago

Snake Bit

getting supplies, but he hasn't brought any gold in from his claim. Both Shultz and Josh Harmon were shot, Josh was found at his claim, shot laying dead by the creek. Jorge Schultz was found dead just off the trail back to his claim" Herb answered. "The men that brought Schulz in said it looked like the killer was trying to hide him in the brush".

I noticed, both Shultz and O'Malley claims are just a little downstream from Dan's claim, and now my stomach was starting to turn.

"Herb, Please do me a favor".

"What's that?".

"If somebody comes in with a bill of sale for Josh's claim or Schultz claim let Jake know, Thanks."

I left the Assayer's Office and headed to the Hutchinson's General Store for some additional supplies. My family runs the General Store but I don't take advantage of the situation, I have my own money. My family does okay, seems like my brother Frank Jr. sees to that, sometimes at the cost of others. I have heard stories about him taking advantage of poor farmer families in the area, but he takes care of Ma.

The Harmen Diner and Bakery are immediately next door to my family's General Store. Josh Harman, his wife Maria, daughter Sara and their 2 sons, run the diner and bakery. Their diner and bakery share a common wall with the family's

Snake Bit

General Store and the Harmens are close to my family. The Diner struggled until Josh added the Bakery giving the business a boost. Josh's widow, Maria was a beautiful mexican lady with black hair and full figure, when she stepped on to the street in Cave Creek every man would watch and admire her. Sara is a younger, more slender version of Maria. Sara's black eyes were mesmerizing. Sara was the middle child of Joshua and Maria and they had two boys, one younger than Sara and one older. I didn't know if I should stop and offer my condolences to the Harman family, I am sure they have enough to worry about.

My mother and sister tried several times to set me up with Josh's daughter, we were close in age. My mother and sister don't seem to understand that I am not ready to settle down. They think, if I found the right woman, maybe I would be ready to settle down. Most women figure me out shortly after meeting me. They want to feel the warmth of the fire but they don't want to live in the fire pit. Sara is beautiful, if I am feeling settled and she ain't spoken for, I will look her up. I am surprised my older brother Eddie hasn't tried to get her attention.

I stepped past the Diner and Bakery and went into my family's store. Katherine or should I say Kate was there by herself. I asked "where is everybody?"

Snake Bit

"Frank and Eddie went to Phoenix for supplies and Ma is next door at Harmen's", "Do you want me to get her?"

"No, leave her be, I can't stay long."

"Did you hear about Josh?"

"I did, I can't let that stand."

"What are you gonna do?"

"Don't you worry about it, just tell Ma I was here." "I need a pound of beans and a box of bullets for my .38 revolver."

"You know you are the only one that buys the .38 caliber bullets"

I started using the Smith & Wesson .38 double action revolver only a few months ago after I heard Billy the Kid killed three men with it. The Story had Billy killing all three before the last man could clear leather. I ordered it through the family store, when it came I tried it out. I put my Colt .45 away and started carrying the .38. Sure enough, you didn't need to pull the hammer back, it comes back when you pull the trigger. The gun likely saved my life once already, I got into a fight with a bank robber named Baxter, he had me down. I could not get my gun clear enough to pull back the hammer, but I was able to get to the trigger and pull it. The bullet killed Baxter and that was that.

Seven

My saddle bags were fully stocked with more ammo than I would take on a hunting trip, something told me I might need it. Finally, on the road and out of town, I started thinking about Dan.

I met Dan Kanton when he came to Dove Valley Ranch to buy a horse from Bill Roberts. Dan liked tall horses and picked out a buckskin gelding with a nice build. The colt was not on my string, I hadn't worked the horse and didn't know much about him. The buckskin coat was from the mustang side but his build was closer to the morgan line. The

Snake Bit

buckskin was almost a hand taller than Queenie and I liked him because like Queenie, he stepped out quickly. The buckskin's step seemed more natural, it was long and quick, Queenie's step was choppy but quick.

Dan took the buckskin for a ride, I rode along to make sure he was sound. We were about a mile off the ranch and Dan was happy with the horse so we decided to turn back. The minute we turned to go home the buckskin tried to take off. Dan pulled in on reins and the horse started to buck, Dan came off landing on his back side but he wasn't hurt. The horse ran back to the ranch. Dan was mad as hell. He jumped on the back of Queenie with me. When we reached the ranch Dan was still unhappy and Bill fit to be tied. Dan chirped "Damn horse made me rip my best shirt". One of the hands caught the buckskin as it came home, and Bill was watching from the ranch house porch. Bill came to the barn mad as hell, he yelled at the ranch hand that was responsible for the string of horses that the buckskin came from. The hand admitted that he hadn't rode the horse out. Bill pulled the string from him, fired him and chased him off the ranch. Bill told Dan, if he still wanted the horse that I would work with him. Dan said he wanted to do the work with me. Bill agreed. Dan wasn't afraid of anything, he said "I am either too dumb or too smart, pick your poison".

Snake Bit

True enough, but he was tough. On occasion, I would think about his statement "either too Dumb or too Smart." I liked it.

We started over from the beginning, we did all of the ground work. When he was ready Dan rode the horse in the big pen without a problem. Dan was happy with the way the horse responded to neck reining, he stopped good. Dan could throw a rope from him, with no problems. We decided to ride the horse off the ranch to see how he reacted. We rode up and down Cave Creek Road with no problem, as long as he could see the barn he was okay. We decided it was time for a longer ride, so we headed west away from the ranch. There was a small valley on the other side of Cave Creek with some mines in the hills on both sides of the valley. When we were about two miles out we turned back and damned if that buckskin didn't blow up again. This time Dan was ready, he sat deep in the saddle, heels down and a strong grip on the saddle horn this time the buckskin couldn't throw him. Dan reined hard to the right, he got the horse turned around heading away from the ranch. The horse settled out and we turned to go back to the ranch and just like that the rodeo was on again. Dan again took control of the horse, and by this point Dan was smoldering. "You won't be going back to the barn any time soon" Dan yelled at the horse. We rode up and down hills, and every time we turned back home the horse tried to break away. We rode that horse until he was dead tired, he finally gave in and then we went home. Dan cooled him down and made sure the horse got grain and water. Bill taught me a great trick, each ranch hand fed and watered his string of horses, making the horse dependent on the ranch hand. We got up early in the morning and did it all again and again for days after that. Then one day Dan took the horse out on his own, everything went well. It seemed Dan and the buckskin had come to terms. I realized that Dan would not be denied, that's a quality I can appreciate. The hours on the trail breaking that horse Dan and I became friends. After it was clear that Dan would keep the buckskin it was time to name him. I came up with the name, Bucky for the obvious reason, he was a buckskin. Dan didn't like that because of his past behavior, he wanted to call him Cuervo after his favorite tequila with a blond color. He insisted on the name Cuervo, but I refused to give in, to this day I call him Bucky.

Time passed quickly, as I was closing in on Dan's claim. At that point, I was about twenty minutes from Dan's claim. I thought I was the only one on the trail, then I twigged to the feeling that I was being watched. I arrived at Dan's claim to find

Snake Bit

him digging at the bend in the creek bed, filling a bucket with dirt.

"Hey bitch" I called out to Dan in a playful tone.

"Hutch what the hell is going on? You are here just in time."

"In time for what" I asked.

"For the panning, let's go inside the tent."

I got off Queenie and tied her to a tent post.

Dan grabbed his bucket of dirt and started into his tent. Dan asked "would you grab the bucket of water?"

As we settled in his tent he asked "Did you see anybody on your way in?" Dan asked.

"No, but I couldn't shake the feeling I was being watched".

"Yae, they are watching, did you hear Joshua Harman was killed" Dan asked?

"Jake told me."

"He wasn't a careful man, he worked out in the open, they saw where he hit paydirt. Check this out" Dan pulled out a mason jar half filled with gold.

"Shit" I gushed "it's got to be over a pound."

"Having this here is dangerous, I got to take this into town tomorrow" Dan added "the way I figure it, I am done here, I easily covered my bet."

"Well that's a short trip for me, I hope you don't mind being trial bait".

Snake Bit

"What do you mean?" Dan looked with a questioning eye.

"One prospector went missing and another was murdered after they left the Assayer's office, with a pocket full of cash. You know about Josh, he was killed at his claim". "I spoke with Marshal Jake, he's worried that there might be more killings." I continued "Your camp might be in a great spot for panning, but it's hard to defend. You're in a narrow part of the canyon. The walls are high enough, one man could ambush the next owner. It will be easy pickins, like snakes in a pit. We need to get this killer"

Dan conceded "you are right". We stopped and pondered the situation for a minute.

"We know something is up, we need to turn the table on the killer or killers" I offered.

"What is your plan?" Dan asked.

"We'll go into town tomorrow like you planned, I will ride a few minutes ahead of you. I will keep an eye on the trail, then I will find a high spot and cover you, if we make it to town, you head to the Assayer's Office to cash in and I will head to the Saloon, they won't make a run at you in town. I will keep a watch from the Saloon, If someone follows you into town I will be watching, I got your back".

Dan questioned "then what?"

Snake Bit

"You head to the General Store after you are done at the Assayer's Office, I will come from the saloon to fill you in on what I saw. You can head over to the Saloon after that, I'll watch from the second story window of the store. Later, I will catch up with you in the hotel and fill you in. The next morning, I will head out early, I'll go towards the ranch just in case I am being watched, then I will double back. I will position myself in the hills above the creek and keep watch and make sure you're not blind sided. What do you think?"

Dan replied "that works for me, you weren't kidding about being bait. My plan was to find some gold and increase the value of the claim and sell it off. I have worked harder than I ever thought I would, but then I never thought I would find this much gold. I have made enough to cover my investment including supplies". Dan continued "While I am in the saloon, I try to find a buyer for this claim."

"The killer or killers will probably overhear you."

"I hope so, then the trap will be set, they will want to steal the claim before I sell it". Dan smiled.

"You could just sell it to them."

"I don't want them to have it, I want some hard working man with a family to feed to have it so he can take care of his family."

Snake Bit

"I understand, and selling it to the killer won't take care of Jake's problem." "If we get back to the claim with no trouble we'll figure out the next step at that time"

"You want to rustle up some dinner while I pan out this last bucket" Dan asked?

"Sure, what do you got?" I asked.

"I got pintos stewing over the fire, add some of that salt pork and chili powder from that box over there" Dan replied.

I chopped the salt pork and added chili powder. I brought enough beef jerky for a five day trip, I guess I won't need all of it, so I grabbed some of the jerky from my bag, chopped it up and added it to the beans. Buster let out a groan, so I threw him a couple of pieces of jerky.

Dan finished panning the last bit of creek sand he pulled from the riverbed "Hutch come take a look at this." Dan's pan held three shiny gold nuggets each the size of a small tooth.

"Holy shit, you hit a honey hole" I chirped.

"Quite Hutch, the hills have ears" Dan scolded then he continued "the bend in the creek slows the water and dirt down long enough for the gold to settle to the button of the creek".

"Where did you learn that?" I asked.

Snake Bit

"I talked to an old miner, he had a claim downstream, he told me. He went to town and never came back".

"Did you catch his name?" I asked

"Old Joe is what the other miners called him?"

"Why do you ask?"

"He was the other minor that was murdered"

"Well" Dan said, after a sigh "I think I've found enough gold, if I can't sell the claim I will walk away and keep these nuggets for good luck."

After winning this Placer Claim in a card game in Wickenburg with three 3s Dan came to believe three was his lucky number so the three gold nuggets fit his story. You know nine could have been his lucky number, we may never know.

The beans were good, we also had some biscuits Winnie packed, we washed it all down with water. We skipped the whisky we wanted to keep our wits about us.

We swapped stories before bedding down. I told Dan what happened between me and Andrea, he just laughed at me. While I was getting into my bed roll, all I could think about was beans before the ride into town, I am sure it will all come back to haunt us in the end.

Eight

The morning sun filled Dan's tent, as I slowly made my way out of my bedroll I realized that Dan was already up and moving. The odor in the tent was awful, damn beans. I opened the flaps and let it air out. I pulled myself together, I noticed Dan brought a bucket of fresh water up from the creek, I used some to wash my face. Dan was a busy beaver, he stoked the camp fire and reheated the

Snake Bit

beans and biscuits for breakfast he put on a pot of coffee. After breakfast we cleaned up camp and Dan locked all his prospecting equipment in his strong box in the tent. We brushed and saddled the horses for the trip to town.

I hit the trail just ahead of Dan, it was mid morning, if it all went well we would be back in town by early afternoon. As soon as we started out my senses were twitching. My stomach started to brew, I could see that the trail started to narrow up ahead, I tapped Queenie in the side very lightly and we quickly moved ahead of Dan and Bucky. Once the trail had narrowed and the canyon walls blocked any escape route, I lifted myself up just off the saddle and let the pressure in my gut release. Shortly after that I heard Dan object "You asshole, what did you do? Shit your pants."

"I don't know, I will have to check at our next stop, you shouldn't have fed me beans" I replied.
At that point I climbed out of the canyon and Dan continued to ride the canyon trail along the creek.

I scanned the ridges for spies and bushwackers, I was relieved not to see any. As I turned east towards town a rider moved on to the trail from the south, he must have been shadowing us from the beginning. Well no need to ride into town ahead of Dan, I went down into the canyon, we rode into town together and I peeled off at the

Snake Bit

saloon while Dan headed to the Assayers office. Dan won his Placer claim with a handful of threes, they came on the deal, he didn't even have to draw any other cards. He somehow got it into his head that three was his lucky number. Dan stepped into the Assayers office to cash in all of his gold except the three nuggets he had panned the night before. Dan asked "what's the price of gold today Herb?"

Herb said "A one ounce gold coin is $20.67, but I can't give you that much for gold dust, the best I can do is $18.00 an ounce. I sell it to the refinery, The refinery melts it into bars, then they send it to Denver or San Francisco to be stamped into coins"

Dan put the mason jar of gold dust on the counter and said "I guess that will work."

Herb weighed Dan's gold dust and cashed him out saying "a little over 17 ounces $310, that is a good haul, watch your back". Dan replied "Thanks Herb, I heard, I will be careful. By the way, do you know anybody that is looking to buy a placer claim, equipment included?". Herb thought for a moment and asked "How much do you need for it?".

Dan hadn't thought about a price until that very moment, he thought about it and said "Well Herb, I won the claim in a poker game. For a good man with a family, I'd sell it for $50 in gold."

Herb asked "Why so low?".

Snake Bit

Dan answered "I have done well with it, all I need is a stake for the next card game. Besides, it ain't worth nothing unless a man is willing to work it and I am not".

Dan put his cash and coins into his pocket and turned to walk out the door. Dan stepped into the fresh spring air and looked around to get his bearings. As Dan walked to the General Store he could feel eyes on him. Across the street the Stranger that followed me and Dan into town watched Dan enter the Hutchinson General Store. After Dan entered the Store I made my way across the street to the General Store.

Snake Bit

Nine

I stepped into the store, and left Buster outside to watch the door. He curled up comfortably on the boardwalk in the shade. Dan was seated next to the window with a cup of coffee. I sat next to him and grunted at my sister Kate "Can I get a cup of coffee too, and make sure Dan pays for his, he's rich now." Kate brought a cup and set it in front of me. Kate said with a little honey in her voice "I bought Dan's coffee". Clearly she is sweet on Dan, they are about the same age but he is far too worldly for her . I looked at her and said "Thanks." Kate moved back

Snake Bit

to the counter to let us talk. There were no customers in the store so we could talk freely. I looked at Dan and started "No reason to wonder, we were followed into town and the same man that followed us had his eyes on you as you stepped out of the Assayer's Office. I only saw one man, but that doesn't mean he don't have friends."

Dan said "sounds like we should change the plan". Dan blew on the hot coffee and continued " After we are done here, I am going to the Barber's for a bath and a shave"

I added with a grin "ya you need it, but so do I". Looking at Dan I asked "how do you want to play it?

Dan took a minute and started "The Stranger has seen us together but he doesn't know that you got my back." He continued "You wait until I get settled in the Barber's before you come in. When I am done I will head to the Hotel, I will get us a couple of rooms in the hotel and leave your key with the clerk." Dan took a sip of his coffee and continued "I will head into the saloon and take a spot at the bar. He won't bother me there but he will be paying attention." Dan paused and said "I started the seed at the Assayer's Office, As the saloon fills up I will act a little sloppy and loosen my lips, I will make

Snake Bit

sure anybody within earshot knows my claim is for sale.   You follow me after you're done at the Barber's, sit away from the bar so you can see the Stranger." "In the morning I'll stay in the hotel and watch your back as you ride out early."

Dan finished his coffee and tipped his hat to Kate behind the store counter.   Kate returned a coquettish smile. Dan stepped out on the boardwalk and Buster stood up, Dan gave Buster a pat on the head and headed towards the Barber Shop.   Dan noticed the Stranger glaring at him from the bar as he made his way.

Dan made a left turn and headed into the Barber Shop.   As he stepped into the Barber Shop he caught the Barber's eye, Dan said "Bath and a shave".   The barber pointed to the back through a curtain, he didn't have to tell Dan he had been there before.   Dan closed the curtain behind him.   In the room behind the curtain there were three wooden tubs arranged from left to right. Just behind each tub about shoulder high there is a wood peg attached to the wall to hang clothes and your gun belt on. A few feet from the tub on the right stood a wood stove made of cast iron. The tubs were oval shaped, with a plank or shelf over the middle of the tub.   The plank was there for modesty and your shaving kit if you had one. Dan settled in the tub on the right as

Snake Bit

the barber made his way into the back room, Dan asked "You got fresh water this morning?"

Barber said "got some heating on the stove, thanks for taking that tub, keeps me from carrying the water too far."

As Dan settled in he faced the curtain and set his gun on the plank. The Barber poured in 2 large buckets of water close to where Dan's feet. The first bucket was hot, he wasn't ready for that but it didn't burn, the second seemed a little cooler and when he poured the third bucket Dan didn't notice a change in the heat. Just as the Barber moved back to the stove for another bucket, Dan heard the Barber Shop door open. Dan picked up his gun and aimed at the curtain. Hutch pulled the curtain open and Dan set his gun back down. Dan barked at Hutch "Close the damn curtain you're letting the cold in".

Hutch, being cautious, took the tub on the left side of the room, that way he wasn't in a straight line with the curtain. The Braber groaned a little but he was happy for the business.

"You two know each other?" the Barber asked.

I sighed and said "I am afraid so".

Dan shot back "Thanks Partner".

Snake Bit

I stopped and took a minute to think about that. I had known Dan for a couple of years by now, I never thought about putting a label on our relationship, I ain't never had a partner before, I like it. Dan was drifter and smarter than most, but I bring the detail to the circumstances. I thought if I ever left Dove Valley for good, Dan wouldn't be bad company.

Dan finished his bath, dried himself off and dressed. Dan looked at the Barber and asked "How about a shave".

The Barber said "Sure, let me put this last bucket of hot water in your friend's tub". The Barber grabbed a couple of small towels, soaked them in water and put them on the stove. He poured Hutch's last bucket of water, walked back to the stove for the now hot towels. He walked through the curtain where Dan had settled into the Barber chair, Dan had his gun across his lap just in case. The Barber draped a large cape over Dan and applied the two hot towels to his face and let them sit for a couple of minutes.

I realized my bath water was cooling quickly, and decided to get out of the bath. I Dressed, and moved to the front of the shop, took a seat and waited for my shave.

Snake Bit

When the Barber was done with Dan, Dan moved to the Door, he looked back at me and said "Show Time" as he stepped out of the Barber Shop. I nodded and said "good luck". Then I moved to the Barber chair.

Ten

Dan crossed the street to the Hotel. The saloon was attached to the Hotel Lobby through an opening in the left wall of the Hotel. Through another opening in the right wall of the Hotel lobby you can find a small dining room with 5 tables for the Hotel guests and town folk. In the Hotel, Dan made his way to the front desk, waking the Clerk he asked for two rooms. He told the Clerk "One for me and another for my partner, he goes by Hutch, he will pick up the key from you later". The Clerk knew Hutch and didn't ask any questions. Dan put his key

Snake Bit

in his pocket and headed upstairs to drop off his gear.

With his gear safely stashed in his room Dan went down stairs. It was about midafternoon when he entered the Saloon from the lobby and headed straight for the bar. Dan looked up to see the big mirror over the bar, and he noticed the Stranger was sitting at a table next to the window. The Stranger had a bottle and one glass in front of him. Dan hoped that meant he didn't have any partners. Dan pushed the front of his hat up and caught the Bartender's attention. The Bartender asked "Can I get you something?".

Dan turned to the Bartender and said "Bottle of Tequila, Cuervo if you got it?"

Bartender said "Sorry fella all we got is whiskey and beer and the beer is warm".

Dan moaned "I'll have a bottle of whiskey and a glass".

Bartender said "That will be $2.00".

Dan went into his pocket and pulled out the money he got from selling his gold to the assayer. Not being coy he made sure everybody in the saloon saw the cash.

Snake Bit

After my shave I went to the Hotel and got my room key. Then I moved through the opening from the Hotel Lobby and went to the bar and asked the Bartender for a Beer. Bartender said "That will be 2 bits, Hutch". I pulled out some silver and put it on the bar. I took the beer and found a table where I could keep one eye on the Stranger and one eye on Dan. Then I settled in for a bit.

After some time the sun started to fade and the Bartender made his way around the room lighting lamps and table candles. Shortly after that cowboys, miners and town folk made their way into the saloon. Shortly after that three ladies came into the Saloon, all the men noticed and it got quiet. There was a redhead and two dark haired girls, all shapely and attractive. These ladies were clearly there for entertainment. The redhead wore a green dress that brought out her eyes. The dress had a deep v in front that exposed a significant amount of her ample breasts. She made her way to a piano at the left side of the bar a couple of tables away from the Stranger. The other two gals were making their way around the saloon flirting and cavorting with the men, hoping to find customers, I am sure. The redhead now at the piano began to play soft and low at first but slowly building. Then she began to sing, and Dan looked up from his bottle and took notice.

Snake Bit

One of the girls left out the backdoor with a cowboy, I recognised him from Dove Valley Ranch, it must be payday.

As the evening moved on Dan made his way to the piano. My guess was to flirt, but to my surprise he began to sing along with the redhead. The two sounded good together. Then Dan sat down on the piano bench with her and started to play. All the while the Stranger kept watch. I had no idea Dan could play piano and sing. After a couple more songs, Dan noticed a few gentlemen gathering around a table, he had a keen eye for a poker game and one was about to start. Dan moved to the poker table and bought in. The table was not far from where the Stranger was set up, so I could keep my eyes on both. Time passed and the saloon was slowly emptying, and I noticed the redhead whispering in Dan's ear. Dan won the next pot and cashed in. The other players complained because Dan left them with little cash. Dan and the redhead made their way through the Hotel Lobby and up the stairs to his room.

I kept an eye on the Stranger for a few more minutes and I headed up to my room. I settled in bed for what I hoped would be a good night's sleep, I knew the next day would be brutal. I was about to drift off when I heard a low moaning coming from

Snake Bit

Dan's room then it went quiet and then I heard it again, it wasn't too hard to figure out what was going on. I turned on to my side and put a pillow over my head and went to sleep.

Eleven

At first light, I heard a noise, not knowing what it was I sprang up in the bed, grabbed my gun and stopped to listen. There it is again I thought, at the same time realizing it was coming from Dan's room and nobody is being hurt, it is the same moan from last night.   I was up so I washed up and got dressed and went down to the dining room for breakfast. Before I left my room, I knocked on the wall between my room and Dan's to signal my departure. Breakfast was steak, eggs, beans and biscuits with coffee to wash it all down. I would need it, it was going to be a long day. Having finished breakfast, I

Snake Bit

headed to the stable to get the day started. Buster was there with Queenie, he kept her company overnight, but he was ready to go. Queenie had just finished a generous bucket grain, so I brushed and saddled her. I noticed Buster was staring me down, so I reached into my saddle bag and came up with a few nice sized pieces of jerky and a day old biscuit, that made Buster happy. I rode west out of town toward cave creek, it was just a short ride and I got there quickly. I found a nice shaded place just off the bank of the creek. I had good cover, I could see if somebody was coming but they would have a hard time seeing me. I got off of Queenie and took up the watch. Within a half hour I saw Dan approach. I made sure he had seen me as he passed by, no reason to startle him. Before mounting Queenie, I checked my gun to make sure it was fully loaded, no reason to think it wouldn't be, just making sure. Today was different, I could feel it, something was in the air. I didn't know what was going to happen but I was ready. After we caught up with Dan, it was a short ride to the claim, less than an hour anyway. When we reached the camp, everything looked like it did when we left 2 days ago. We got off our horses, I took Queenie and Cuervo and tied them to a palo verde tree a few feet away. All of a sudden Dan yelled out "Hutch come here!".

Snake Bit

At that moment Buster started growling, I looked at Buster and asked, not expecting an answer "What do you see Buster?". I moved towards Dan's tent and caught some movement out of the corner of my right eye. I turned to look and saw the Stranger on the other side of the creek. He had his gun in his right hand, ready to shoot. I hit the ground behind the tent as he fired on me. I heard the bullet hit the dirt behind me. Dan yelled "What the hell is going on out there?" I whispered back "Hit the ground, we got company.".

Dan whispered back "I am down, how many?.

I answered "I only see one, it's your stalker."

While we were sharing intelligence, I made my way around to the other side of the tent. Gathering myself but staying low I heard another shot, it tore a small hole through Dan's tent. Now, I could see the Stranger, but being right handed I would have to expose myself to get a clear shot, I thought what the Hell.

I Stepped out and took a shot, but so did he. His shot hit me high on the left shoulder. My shot must have missed. With my double action revolver, I got off a second shot before he could reset his hammer and this one hit him solid in the right shoulder. He fell backwards but he still had his gun

Snake Bit

in his hand. Buster crossed the creek and was on the Stranger before he could move, Buster bit into his right hand, the Stranger tried to shake him off but Buster wouldn't let go. Finally the Stranger dropped the gun. I scrambled across the creek and grabbed the Strangers gun. I yelled out to Dan "All Clear".

Dan came out of the tent and crossed the creek. I could tell Dan was pissed off. Dan put his boot on the Stranger's wound and ground into it.

Dan barked "Who the Hell are you and what the hell are you doing here?".

The Stranger, grimacing, said "Go to Hell".

Dan pushed harder and "Said looks like you'll make it there first".

With more pressure came more pain, it became unbearable and the Stranger gave up. He yelled "All right, alright I will tell you if you let up".

Dan pushed harder and the Stranger let out another yell and Dan let up. Asking "you better get to talking, who the hell are you?

The Stranger was white as a ghost with pain, but he wouldn't die from this injury. Finally he said "My name is Blake Haggard and I work for the

Snake Bit

Phoenix Mining Company". "I've been hired to chase all of you Placer Miners off."

Dan replied "You didn't have to kill them. You thought you could steal the claims get away with it, you piece of shit"

I stepped in and asked "Did you kill Josh Harmen?"

Haggard said "I ain't telling you another thing".

Standing over him, I pulled my gun out and pointed at Haggard's head and said "speak up or forever hold your piece." I read that somewhere.

Haggard said "You ain't gonna shoot me you ain't pulled back your hammer back".

I pulled the gun to the left and fired, missing his ear. Haggard pissed himself. I laughed and said "This is double action 38, it doesn't have to be cocked to shoot. It doesn't have the knock down power of your .45, but I can shoot twice as fast."

As I was standing over Haggard, I noticed the blood was dripping on him and I knew it wasn't his. With the heat of the moment cooling down I realized it was my blood as I started to get dizzy.

Dan asked me "are you okay?"

Snake Bit

"It stings like a son of bitch, feels like I got bit by rattler"

"We better take care of that."

Haggard said "I need help too."

Dan looked at Haggard and said "You're next, yah we'll fix you up so you can face the gallows."

After Dan dressed my wound we patched up Haggard, then tied his hands and feet. We found his horse tied to a palo verde tree up the trail a bit. We searched his saddle bags and found enough evidence to hang him, including Josh Harmen's claim.

Dan was done with his prospecting, he cleaned up his tent and left all of his mining equipment in the trunk. He said "I don't want to carry this crap, I will leave all of this to the next owner, he'll need it."

We put Haggard on his horse and tied his hands to his saddle horn and we headed back to town. We rode straight to Marshal Compton's office. The cell Rice Rogers was in was now vacant so Haggard had a new home until the County Sheriff came and took him to Phoenix. We turned over all of the evidence we pulled from Haggard's saddle. Using that evidence we told Marshal Compton the story as we knew it.

Snake Bit

Twelve

After this week, I feel like I am a lucky man. Caught a killer and lived to tell. All a man really needs is a good horse, a good saddle and a good dog to keep you company on the long dusty trial. Any more than that can weigh man down. The next morning I caught up with Dan in the Hotel dining room. He was just sitting down for breakfast so I joined him. We both ordered steak, eggs, beans, biscuits and coffee. It is good to have a partner to share the trail with.

I asked "What's next for you?".

Dan took a deep breath and said "Don't rightly know yet, haven't given it much thought, maybe I will stay in town one more night and play some poker.

We ate breakfast in relative silence although I did notice the red headed woman from the other night watching Dan. I quietly said "Dan you either have an admirer or you made an enemy".

Dan said, matching my tone "I know, I sent her to heaven at least three times last night".

I said "I know she is a moaner and you all kept me awake, that might be a reason for you to stay another night".

Dan looked up from his steak with a grin and asked "What's next for you?".

"I am heading back to the ranch to check in. With summer around the corner I am hoping to go to the high country for some cooler weather".

"You worried about facing Bill?".

"Maybe a little, but a man doesn't run from his problems, besides I think Andrea wouldn't tell Bill. She doesn't want to disappoint him any more than I do".

Before leaving town for the ranch, I stopped by the family store to visit my mother. She was not happy to see my torn shirt with the blood stain on my left sleeve. Ma came to attention and demanded "What did you do?"

"I am okay, it's just a graze, you should see the other guy".

She could see that I was okay but she was not happy. She looked at me and said "You damn well better be more careful." Then as an afterthought she asked "We missed you at Andrea's graduation party where were you?".

"I had some business, helping Dan with his gold claim".

Snake Bit

"That's how you got shot. You need to stay clear of him, he'll get you in trouble. Where are you going now? Will we see you this summer?"

"HeadingBack to the ranch, I don't know I am hoping to get out of the summer heat".

Sometimes talking to Ma is more like an inquisition. But, the one time that I didn't take the time to visit might be the last chance I had. Buster and I headed to the stable to get Queenie, she was about done eating her grain. I brushed and saddled her. Queenie, Buster and I headed out of town for the ranch.

About a quarter mile out of town I heard a rider coming up fast from behind, I didn't think anybody was after me. I looked back to see Dan Kanten ride up beside me.

"I thought you were staying in town?".

"Well you know women, they get too clingy and those redheads smell like piss".

I nearly fell off Queenie laughing. We rode the rest of the way to the ranch in silence. Sometimes nothing else needs to be said.

We rode through the west gate of the ranch and headed for my cabin. We unsaddled, brushed and watered Queenie and Cuervo. With that done we put the horses in the stall next to my cabin.

Ric Robertson came running down from the big house, out of breath he mumbled "Pa wants to see you at the house".

"I'll wash up and be there directly".

Ric turned and went back to the house.

Dan asked "you think you're in trouble?"

Snake Bit

"I sure the hell hope not".

"I will wait here".

"You chicken shit".

"What? I got no worries"

"Then come with me, he might pull his punches if you are there".

"Alright, let's go".

We walked up to the house, it was a short walk but seemed like it took forever. We stepped up to the door and knocked.

We heard Bill yell "come on in".

I said to Dan "no hint of anger".

We stepped into the house, and then stepped immediately to the right into Bill's office. The office was a bedroom when the house was first built. Bill was sitting behind his big pine desk he had made in Mexico. The Ranch house started out as a small adobe shack, just a kitchen/family area and a bedroom. The home was expanded with pine logs around the adobe shack, so the office was cool with summer coming on. The Ranchhouse has a handsome pine logged exterior, all to the timbers brought in from the northern part of the territory.

Bill said "I saw you boys ride in, how did it go with the Gold claim?"

I started "Well, Dan ain't a prospector anymore and we caught a killer to boot." Dan added "made a little money, had some good clean fun".

Bill said "You will have to tell me the whole story at dinner tonight. Hutch, I asked you up here to talk about another problem".

Snake Bit

I took a deep breath and a sigh of relief, a dinner invitation, that cleared the air, I guess he can't be too mad. I asked "What's on your mind?".

Bill said "Leslie Graham was out hunting a bear that's been killing livestock in the Payson area, he cornered the bear. The bear wasn't having any of that. Before Les could shoot the bear it attacked his horse. Les was thrown clear and the bear escaped but Les was hurt pretty bad". Bill paused then added "he needs help with his stock while he is laid up. I know it ain't fair to ask but if you don't have any plans, he could surely use your help, what do you think?"

I thought about it for about one second and said "I was planning on a high country trip this summer, I can leave tomorrow morning".

Dan spoke up "You want some company?"

I said "suits me just fine".

To be continued...

Watch for the next Hutch story

"Bear Down"

Snake Bit

Snake Bit

About the Author:

Kelly Goodrich was born in Indio California as a young boy he played Cowboys and Indians in the deserts surrounding the family home.

Later the family moved to the Santee/Lakeside area of San Diego County. Santee/Lakeside was a fast growing area with a mix of rural and suburban living. While living in a subdivision it was only a short bike ride to the neighborhood horse stables. After school Kelly and his brothers would head to the stables, for five dollars they could rent a horse for an hour. If their pockets were empty they could clean out a few stalls and earn an hour's ride.

As the area developed the trails were gobbled up by new subdivisions, eventually the stables closed and families with their horses moved further east into Lakeside and Alpine.

Somewhere along the way the family bought a white thirteen hand pony named Joker. The trails were limited so most of the saddle time with Joker took place in a large corral that was about a hundred feet by two hundred feet and served as the manure dump. Joker would allow them to get on bare back, but after about ten or fifteen minutes he would throw them to the ground and run off leaving them in the sometimes fresh manure. Lucky for the boys, the corral was softened by sand and the horse manure from the cleaned stalls. Eventually Joker was sold as the boys went on to high school.

After High School, Kelly moved to the Phoenix area where he attended community college and later went to Arizona Tech to be trained as a computer programmer. Well into his programming career Kelly began to compete in a shooting sport called Practical Pistol with his brother Mike. After a time Kelly realized that his wife Laurie had no interest in Practical Pistol and the time they spent apart was trying. Laurie suggested horseback riding and Kelly was up for that.

Over time the occasional horseback ride turned into a pastime. Laurie bought Levi's Blue Eye a paint horse with one blue eye, she called him Bluee. Bluee was born on the ranch where he was purchased and had no papers; to look at Bluee you could see qualities of both the American Quarter Horse and the very popular Arabian Horse. Kelly often said he had the body of a Quarter Horse and the heart and head of an Arabian; the last part about the head was not always a compliment. Kelly hit the jackpot when he had the chance to buy Pepper Me Red a registered Quarter Horse mare for a smoking deal. He shortened Pepper Me Red to "Red". Pepper me Red was offered to Kelly for the sum of six hundred dollars, even at the time a ridiculously low price. Red was four years old and wild, she had been trapped in a snow drift in Colorado, she had lost a considerable amount of weight. Red's condition made her docile and easy to handle. Kelly saw to her regular feedings, she grew strong and looked forward to the attention. Kelly paid attention to Red, making her easy to train. Red and Bluee both looked forward to trail Rides and team penning. Red's fast acceleration also made her a good header or heeler

Snake Bit

in the roping arena; she could put the roper in the perfect position to throw the rope. Kelly's roping skills were limited so Red didn't get the opportunity she deserved when it came to roping. Red was also sure footed on roundups. The trail rides with friends kicked Kelly's imagination into high gear, the hutch stories were inspired by those trail rides. From BumbleBee to Seven Springs to Dry Beaver Creek. The incredibly beautiful and dangerous terrain can inspire the simplest soul. The Hutch stories were first outlined around the fire pit back at the ranch after those long trail rides.

Levi's Blue Eye passed in June of 2007 and Pepper Me Red went to the great pasture in the summer of 2014. Sadly, both Red and Bluee have found that big range in the sky where all of their needs will be met. Kelly has been training a new mare, her name is Pepe's Golden Peach, we call her Peaches.

Kelly wrote a Poem for Red shortly after her passing called "One Horse". You can find it on the last pages. All horsemen and cowboys will understand the sentiment.

"There are many trails ahead and Arizona is full of inspiration for the open eye and a longing heart."

Kelly M. Goodrich

I am not a poet, hell I am not even a writer, I just like to tell stories. Sometimes a poem can say it all.

One Horse

We were standing there, staring at an empty
stall
The vet gave us the bad news, and he made
the call
The Cowboy pushed up the brim of his Hat
With a Tear in his eye he Began to Speak

A Cowboy is a Lucky Man if he can count
among his Treasures
One Saddle, One Dog, an One Horse

A Gun don't owe you nothing, if it shoots
straight
But a good Saddle will earn its Keep
With a Horn strong enough to dally any Bull
The Stirrups and Cantel will hold you in your
Seat

A Cowboy is a Lucky Man if he can count
among his Treasures

Snake Bit
One Saddle, One Dog, an One Horse

A good Dog will always be at your Side
He'll work your stock, and stand midnight
Watch
He'll look at you with Love, Loyalty, and Pride

A Cowboy is a Lucky Man if he can count
among his Treasures
One Saddle, One Dog, an One Horse

But, today we say our last Goodbye to my
trusted Mare
She wasn't always agreeable, but she always
met the Task
From a Dusty Cattle Drive to a Drunken
Midnight Ride
She always had my Back

A Cowboy has had a Hell of a Ride if he Counts
among his Treasures
**One Good Saddle, One Good Dog and One
Good Horse**

Snake Bit

Made in the USA
Middletown, DE
29 October 2023

41510630R00057